PUFFIN BOOKS

Dad, Me and
the Dinosaurs

Dad, Me and the Dinosaurs

Jenny Koralek

Illustrated by
Doffy Weir

PUFFIN BOOKS

To Luke – J. K.
Barny, do you remember the dinosaurs' growls? – D. W.

PUFFIN BOOKS

Published by the Penguin Group
Penguin Books Ltd, 27 Wrights Lane, London W8 5TZ, England
Penguin Putnam Inc., 375 Hudson Street, New York, New York 10014, USA
Penguin Books Australia Ltd, Ringwood, Victoria, Australia
Penguin Books Canada Ltd, 10 Alcorn Avenue, Toronto, Ontario, Canada M4V 3B2
Penguin Books (NZ) Ltd, Private Bag 102902, NSMC, Auckland, New Zealand

Penguin Books Ltd, Registered Offices: Harmondsworth, Middlesex, England

First published in 1998
3 5 7 9 10 8 6 4

Text copyright © Jenny Koralek, 1998
Illustrations copyright © Doffy Wier, 1998
All rights reserved

The moral right of the author/illustrator has been asserted

Typeset in Bembo Schoolbook

Printed in Hong Kong by Midas Printing Limited

British Library Cataloguing in Publication Data
A CIP catalogue record for this book is available from the British Library

ISBN 0–140–38700–5

Our baby cried a lot before his tooth
came through.

And Mum was tired.

Dad took down my coat and said,
"I know what, my lovely Lilly!
We'll jump on the bus to Piccadilly!"

1

But we didn't jump.
We waited.
We waited a long time.
I hopped and skipped on the
pavement, but Dad stood in the
queue and tapped his foot.

At last the bus came. We sat in the front seat at the top.

Dad said, "I know what, Lilly mine! To row a boat would just be fine. We'll go to the park and to the Serpentine!"

But when we got to the Serpentine, there was no boat.

And it began to rain.

6

Dad turned our collars up and
sighed.

"Ohhh! Never mind! I know what,
my darling Lil!
The dinosaurs will give us a thrill."

And he waved to a taxi to take us
out of the rain, over the bridge and to
the museum.

In the museum, the dinosaurs were
kept in the dark. Dark and tall, and
near. Not small and papery, not small
on a page in a book that I can shut

when I like . . . Too
near, too tall, too dark,
too scary. And they
growled in their throats.

"It's only a tape," said Dad. "Don't
be frightened, Lilly my sweet.
I thought this museum would be a
treat!"

"D-d-d-d-dad!" I croaked. "G-g-g-
get me out of here!"

"I know what!" said Dad. "It's time
for dinner, not dinosaurs!"

But we didn't have dinner.

Dad patted my hand and said,
"Sorry, my honey.
I've very nearly run out of money.
We'll have just a sandwich or two.
Because of that taxi my pennies
are few."

But I didn't have one sandwich, let alone two.

I peeled back the bread. Mashed up in the egg was some stuff I just won't ever eat!

"Oh dear!" said Dad. "This day is a mess.
I ought to remember you
    never eat cress!
I'd buy you a drink but
    the drinks are all fizzy.
I know what –"

"No, Dad," I said. "*I* know what! Let's take the bus home. There's some pepperoni in the fridge and a drink for me that isn't fizzy, some hot tea for you and perhaps a crumpet!

"And then we will line up all my toys on the floor through the kitchen to the very front door. You can sit in your chair and I will lean my back against your knees and admire the grand parade!"

That's what we did.

The bus came at once.

The rain stopped raining.

There was pepperoni in the fridge
and some apple juice for me.

Dad toasted some crumpets and
drank his hot tea.

We laid out all my toys in a long, long line.

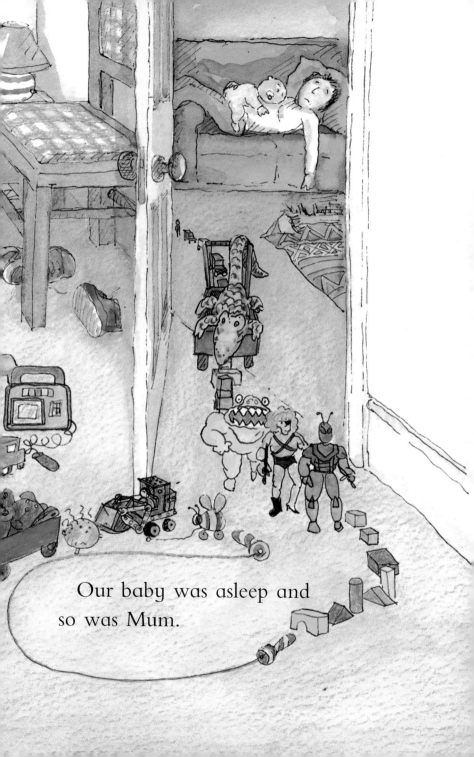

Our baby was asleep and
so was Mum.

My day out with Dad was fine,
just fine.

Also available in First Young Puffin

WHAT STELLA SAW
Wendy Smith

Stella's mum is a fortune-teller who always gets
things wrong. But when football-mad Stella starts
reading tea-leaves, she seems to be right every time!
Or is she . . .?

THE DAY THE SMELLS WENT WRONG
Catherine Sefton

It is just an ordinary day, but Jackie and Phil can't
understand why nothing smells as it should. Toast
smells like tar, fruit smells like fish, and their school
dinners smell of perfume! Together, Jackie and Phil
discover the cause of the problem . . .

DUMPLING
Dick King-Smith

Dumpling wishes she could be long and
sausage-shaped like other dachshunds. When a
witch's cat grants her wish, Dumpling becomes
the longest dog ever.